WHAT DO SMURFS DO ALL DAY ?

WHAT DO SMURFS DO ALL DAY?

by Peyo

BEGINNER BOOKS

A Division of Random House, Inc.

What do Smurfs do all day?

Papa Smurf says,
"Get out of bed!
It's time to get up,
you sleepyhead."

Smurfs brush their teeth
and wash their faces.
They scrub their necks
and other places.

Then they march
to breakfast
on fast feet . . .

. . . and eat and eat and eat.

And then, of course,
the Smurfs clean up.

They wash the dishes.

They mop the floors.

And then it's time
to go outdoors.

Every day
Smurfs like to play.

They like to hide
behind a bush.
They swing on swings.
They pull and push.

Smurfs love to pull.

They pull, pull, pull.

They dive in pools.

They splash about.

They swim and float
and then climb out.

Smurfs go to school.

They read.

They write.

Some spell quite well
and some not quite.

Then after school
they sing, they toot.

They clap their hands.
They howl and hoot.

They love to play.

And when they're through,

they work!

They all have jobs to do.

They stitch and sew,
they bake a cake.

They write a poem.

They hoe and rake.

They lift and lug.

They build and fix.

They scrape and paint.

They stir and mix.

What else do they do?

They snooze.

They sneeze.

And some play jokes.

They like to tease.

They laugh a lot.

Most days they're glad.

Sometimes they cry.

Sometimes they're sad.

Smurfs yell and shout!
Sometimes they mumble.
When they get mad
they grouch and grumble.

Some ride.

Some chase.

Some like to race.

Smurfs like to finish
in first place.

They throw and catch.

They hit the ball.

They ski and skate.

Sometimes they fall.

They run, they jump.

Smurfs love to tumble.

They pass and kick.

Sometimes they fumble.

They follow the leader.
They race about
until at last
they're all tired out.

And when their busy day is through,

they hop in bed, like me and you.

Then all night long,

what do they do...?

Smurfs dream their dreams.

They count their sheep.

They toss and turn

and snore . . . and sleep.